NO MORE SPANISH!

GET READY FOR MORE GaBí!

NO MORE SPANISH!

by Marisa Montes

illustrated by Joe Cepeda

> That's Gabí. As in Ga-BEE. With an
> accent. Not Gabi. 'Cause that's the way
> she likes it. Oh, and it does NOT rhyme with
> blabby! And she does NOT talk too much!

A
LITTLE APPLE
PAPERBACK

SCHOLASTIC INC.
New York Toronto London Auckland Sydney
Mexico City New Delhi Hong Kong Buenos Aires

No part of this work may be reproduced in whole or in part, or stored in
a retrieval system, or transmitted in any form or by any means, electronic,
mechanical, photocopying, recording, or otherwise, without written
permission of the publisher. For information regarding permission, write to
Scholastic Inc., Attention: Permissions Department, 557 Broadway,
New York, NY 10012.

ISBN 0-439-47522-8
Text copyright © 2004 by Marisa Montes
Illustrations copyright © 2004 by Scholastic Inc.
SCHOLASTIC, LITTLE APPLE, and associated logos are trademarks
and/or registered trademarks of Scholastic Inc.

12 11 10 9 8 7 6 5 4 3   5 6 7 8 9/0

Printed in the U.S.A.   40
First printing, February 2004

Para Mami y Papi:
Rubén and Mary Montes.
To Papi for instilling in me
a love, respect, and pride for
my Puerto Rican heritage;
and to Mami for impressing upon me
the power of languages.
— M.M.

For Monet
— J.C.

Acknowledgments

Special thanks to those who helped me make Chapter One of this book as realistic as possible: Carmen T. Bernier-Grand, children's author; Stacey Bickell, English as a Second Language (ESL) teacher at Wells Middle School in Houston, Texas; and Katherine Flores, Upper Grade Title 1-Reading Specialist at Cambridge Elementary School in Concord, California.

Thanks also to my critique group — Susan Middleton Elya and Raquel Victoria Rodriguez — for your insight and ideas, and especially to Corinne Hawkins for helping me identify and flesh out the theme of this book.

Finally, thanks to my aunt, Dr. Carmín Montes Cumming, for being my Spanish consultant and for so patiently reviewing all my manuscripts. And a huge thank-you to my editor, Maria S. Barbo, for always including me in every aspect of the publishing process.

— M.M.

CONTENTS

UNO
CHAPTER 1
"THIS IS MY FAMILY"

"Gabí?" Mr. Fine, my third-grade teacher, called for my attention.

Mr. Fine knows I like people to say my name "Ga-BEE," so that's how he always says it. That way, it rhymes with *coquí*, a cool little tree frog from Puerto Rico. That's where Mami and Abuelita, my grandma, are from.

"Would you like to introduce your family now?" Mr. Fine asked.

This month, the kids in my class get to bring our families to school and interview them. We interview one family a day. It's

part of our new project called "All About Me."

"Sure, Mr. Fine!" I rushed to the front of the room.

I was *soooo* excited about having the class meet *mi familia,* I had hardly slept the night before.

I've always been super proud of my family. So I wrote up *montones* — oodles — of perfect interview questions for them. And I practiced for two weeks in front of the mirror.

"I'm, umm . . . Maritza Gabriela Morales Mercado," I said. "Gabí for short. And this is my family, the Morales-Mercados."

Even though everybody knew us, we were supposed to introduce ourselves first. Mr. F said it was good practice for speaking in public.

My family stood in the back of the room, waiting to be introduced. When I waved to them, they marched in one long line toward the front of the class.

Abuelita came first. She looked so pretty with her hair in a twisty knot the way I like it.

Then came Papi in a suit and a green bow tie that matched his eyes. His hair is a little darker brown than mine, but it's just as wavy. I was glad to see he hadn't forgotten to take off his white lab coat before he left work.

Giggles broke out in the class.

My head snapped toward the other kids. What was so funny?

Then I saw what was happening.

Mami was having trouble walking.

You won't *believe* this! My four-year-old brother, Miguelito, had his face stuck to her skirt! Mami tried to unwrap Miguelito's arms from her leg and walk at the same time. But Miguelito hung on tight — like he was super-glued to her side. He squirmed and mumbled

4

something that
sounded like
"Teenagers!"

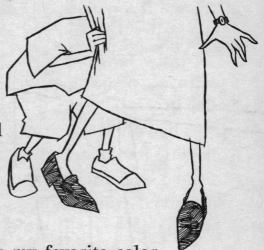

The class gig-
gled even more.

My face turned
the color of my
trusty cowgirl
boots — bright
red.

Red is usually my favorite color.
But NOT when it's on my face!

Ever since he turned four, Miguelito has
thought all kids my age and older were
teenagers. Even though we were still third
graders and wouldn't be teenagers for a
long, long time.

To Miguelito, teenagers were *way* cool. So
cool that he was afraid to look at them. But
I didn't want my whole class knowing that.

Papi helped Mami peel off Miguelito.
Then he carried him to his chair. Miguelito

stuck his face in Papi's neck and wrapped his legs around him.

"*Siéntate, Miguelito.*" Papi tried to pull Miguelito away and make him sit in his own chair.

Miguelito wouldn't let go. He stuck to Papi like a magnet to a fridge.

Now my whole head sizzled. *¡Qué bochorno!* How embarrassing!

"He's so shy!" someone whispered.

¡Caracoles! I thought as I pressed my lips together. *Doggone it!*

This was NOT how I'd planned to start my interview!

DOS
CHAPTER 2
BURRITOS AND TAQUITOS!

Miquelito kept squirming and clinging to Papi. Mami and Papi tried to calm Miguelito in Spanish. They whispered, but to me, they sounded like they were talking through mega-loud speakers. Their voices blared in my ears.

The class leaned forward in their desks. I could feel their eyes on us.

I've always been so proud that my family and I speak two languages. But today, I wished they would stop speaking Spanish. I just wanted to get on with my interview.

But for some weird reason, I felt as if I had to explain to the class.

"Um . . ." I cleared my throat. "My family, uhhh . . . we always speak Spanish to one another. Even though we all speak English," I added quickly. "Well, everyone except my grandmother, I mean. Abuelita is visiting us from Puerto Rico and hasn't learned English yet."

I fumbled with my note cards. "Speaking Spanish with one another is a really strict rule my parents have so we'll never forget how to speak it. Mami says language is power, so it's important to speak more than one language."

I grinned real big at Mami when I said that. Mami nodded and smiled.

Before I could say anything else, Johnny Wiley raised his hand.

I rolled my eyes. *What now?* I thought.

Johnny Wiley is Public Enemy *Número Uno* and my biggest pain.

"Yes, Johnny?" said Mr. Fine.

Johnny stood. "I just wanted to say that I know some Spanish, too."

"Really?" Mr. F's bushy eyebrows bounced above his glasses.

"Yeah, Mr. F, listen to this: *Burritos* and *taquitos*! *¡Fajita grande! ¡Cha-cha-cha!*" Johnny looked all proud, like he was some sort of rocket scientist.

"That's enough, Johnny," Mr. F said. "Let's talk after class." He was using his serious voice, but when he turned to me, he winked. "Gabí, please go on."

Johnny sat down. His best friend, Billy Wong, patted him on the back.

Heat rushed to my face. I turned to Mami and Papi. Papi was shaking his head. Mami was smiling gently, the way she does when Miguelito has said something silly. They didn't seem annoyed by Johnny's dopey comments.

But I was. My fingers fumbled with my note cards again.

I glanced at my best friend, Devin Suzuki. Devin speaks Spanish really well because she used to live in Panama. She gave her light brown hair a tug.

That's our secret signal. It was supposed to make me feel better.

It didn't.

I cleared my throat again. Then I looked back at the class . . . and froze. The first thing I saw was Johnny and Billy, grinning like chimpanzees.

I scrunched up my toes. I wanted to run over there and teach those bad boys a good lesson.

But I knew I had to behave while Mr. F and my parents were watching.

I looked down at the note cards in my hand. *¡Caracoles! — Yikes! Where was the first card? Where was Question One?*

The moment I started to shuffle through the cards, they flew from my hands and scattered all over the floor. Quick, quick, quick, I grabbed up all the cards.

But now, the cards were out of order!

I felt *más perdida que una cucaracha en un*

baile de gallinas, as Mami would say. More lost than a cockroach at a chicken dance. Everyone was staring at me, but I couldn't speak.

As if things weren't bad enough, Sissy Huffer (Royal Pain *Número Dos*) shook her prissy yellow curls at me. She pretended to look really sad.

"Geez Louise, Gabí," she whispered, all sickly sweet. "Do you have stage fright?"

I looked away from her. But before I did, I saw Sissy smile.

¡Caracoles! What a mess! I wanted to run, hide, disappear! This was supposed to be my big day.

Everything would have been fine if my family had been speaking English.

Now Spanish was ruining everything!

TRES
CHAPTER 3
IN SPANISH!

"Gabí," Mr. Fine said after he had helped me sort my note cards, "are you ready?"

I stepped behind Mami and took a deep breath. "This is my *mami* . . . uh . . . mother, Ms. Isabel Mercado. My . . . um . . . mom is a lawyer."

It felt weird to call Mami "mom." I've always called my parents Mami and Papi. But somehow, I couldn't make my mouth say anything in Spanish now.

Next, I stood behind Papi. "This is my father, Dr. Antonio Morales." I forced a grin.

"Pa — uh . . . my dad is . . . um . . . a mad scientist."

Some kids gasped. Some kids' mouths opened wide.

Devin gave her hair a double tug. That means "Good job!"

My other best friend, Jasmine Lange, crossed her eyes. She always does that when she likes something.

I put my hand on Miguelito's head. "This is my little brother, Miguelito."

The moment I said that, Miguelito began to crawl under Papi's armpit. He looked like a cat trying to force his head through a tiny mouse hole.

The class giggled.

"He's only four," I said. "And he's kind of . . . shy with strangers."

I didn't want to tell them that Miguelito thought they were teenagers.

I stepped real quick behind Abuelita.

"This is my grandmother, Señora Gabriela Beatriz Gutiérrez Mercado. Like I said before, she's visiting with us from Puerto Rico. You can call her . . . S-Señora Mercado," I added, stumbling on the Spanish part.

"Thank you for the introductions, Gabí,"

said Mr. Fine. "Would anyone like to ask Gabi's family any questions?"

My jaw dropped. I stared at Mr. F. I was just about to ask, "What about *my* questions?"

That's when Johnny Wiley's hand shot up. He wanted to know if Papi had ever blown up his lab.

Papi said no, he hoped not. "It was still there when I left this afternoon. But I spilled some chemicals once. And I came home smelling like rotten eggs."

All the girls said, "Eee-oooo! Gross!" Sissy Huffer scrunched up her nose. But the boys said, "Cool! Way to go!" and held up their thumbs.

Billy Wong wanted to know if Mami had ever helped put away big criminals. Mami told him she wasn't that kind of lawyer.

"I help people stand up for their rights under the U.S. Constitution," she said.

There were lots of "Oo-ooos" and "Oh-hhhs" when Mami said that.

I stood up straight and grinned. I began to feel much better.

I'm really proud of Mami. She's doing what I want to do someday. She protects people from bullies and bad guys.

I want to stamp out evil, too. But I'm going to do it by becoming a secret agent for a big government agency.

Mami fights bad guys by using her head. I like to fight bad guys with my spunky feet. And my cowgirl boots. But that usually gets me into trouble with a capital T-R-O-U-B-L-E.

Sissy raised her hand. "Would you please tell us about Puerto Rico, Señora Mercado?" she asked Abuelita.

I glared at Sissy. What a question! Abuelita could talk all day about Puerto Rico. And, of course, since Abuelita doesn't understand English, I'd have to translate.

Everyone waited for Abuelita to answer. She looked at me, waiting for me to tell her what Sissy had said.

I usually don't mind translating. In fact, I've always liked it. It's fun, and it makes me feel important.

But right now, I was dreading opening my mouth and having Spanish pour out. I didn't want to give Johnny *or* Billy more reasons to make fun of me like they usually did.

All the good feelings I'd had about Mami

began to disappear. I whispered to Abuelita what Sissy had asked.

"*¿Cómo?*" Abuelita said, leaning forward. "*No oigo.*"

She couldn't hear me. So I stepped closer and whispered a little louder.

Abuelita shook her head. "*Todavía no te oigo, Gabrielita.*"

I took a deep breath and spoke so she could hear me.

Abuelita smiled at Sissy. "*Ah, qué linda.*" I wasn't about to tell snooty Sissy that she was adorable. I waited until Abuelita said something I could translate. It didn't take long. She rattled off all sorts of things about Puerto Rico.

She went on and on and on. It felt like forever! I had to keep jumping in when she took a breath so I could repeat what she said in English. It was kind of like playing jump rope and having to wait until the rope was up high so I could jump in without getting tangled in the rope.

Johnny and Billy started working their hands like puppet mouths and grinning like chimps. They were making fun of Spanish!

The more Abuelita spoke, the more embarrassed I got. The words didn't make sense anymore.

The class had tons of questions for her. And I had to translate ALL of them. In the front of the room. *In Spanish!*

Even though I'd spoken Spanish all my life, *today* it felt klutzy and clunky. Like my tongue was all twisted up in my mouth.

And everything was getting all mixed-up in my brain, too. I wasn't sure what would come out the next time I opened my mouth — Spanish or English or . . . *ay, ay, ay* . . . Spanglish!

I wanted to stop speaking Spanish. And I wanted to stop *right now*. In fact, I never wanted to speak Spanish again. *Ever.*

But Abuelita made Puerto Rico sound so interesting that the class kept asking question after question. They weren't giving *me* a chance to ask any of my perfect interview questions. Everything was going wrong!

Mami and Papi didn't seem to notice. They were smiling and nodding.

Then Abuelita said something totally humiliating. *No way* was I going to tell the class about that! Instead, I turned to Mami.

I was about to ask her a question when Johnny Wiley raised his hand.

"What did your grandmother say, Ga-*BEE*?" Johnny asked.

¡Caracoles! See why he's Public Enemy *Número Uno*?

Mr. F smiled. "Go ahead, Gabí. It sounded interesting."

Obviously, he had no idea what Abuelita had said.

I sighed. "She said that *tapones* — traffic jams — in the big cities of Puerto Rico used to be really bad. Cars could sit for an hour or more and not move an inch."

I turned to Mami again. "Now *I'd* like to ask some questions."

Then — *you won't believe this!* —

Miguelito peeked out from under Papi's armpit and yelled in perfect English, "No, wait, there's more!"

He pulled away from Papi and looked at me. "That's not *all* Abuelita said. Remember, Gabí? She said that one time we went to visit her and got stuck in a *tapón*. You had to go to the bathroom so bad, you tinkled in your pants in the car."

I practically fell over backward. *Why did he choose* NOW *to talk?*

The class almost rolled on the floor howling.

"Ga-BEE wet her pants!" Johnny yelled.

¡Caracoles! I wanted to disappear and never come back!

25

CUATRO
CHAPTER 4
NO MORE SPANISH!

After his comment, Miguelito sat in his own chair next to Papi. But he covered his face with his hands so he wouldn't have to look at the class.

At least Abuelita was done talking, and Mami and Papi answered my questions in English. But I was so embarrassed I hardly asked them any of my perfect questions.

I'll forever remember that interview as the most horrible, embarrassing, miserable experience of my life. But Mami and Papi thought it went great.

"Gabita," Papi said when we left school, "Mami and I thought it would be fun if we all went out to an early dinner. To celebrate our interview."

Celebrate!? See what I mean? Trust me, celebrating was NOT what I wanted to do. Hiding under the bed with my cat, Tippy, maybe. But definitely *not* celebrating. Why didn't my family get that?

So instead of going home, Papi drove us to our favorite pizza place. When we walked into the restaurant, my family was laughing. They were going on and on about how cute Miguelito had been during the interview.

The restaurant was tiny and dark. Since it was early, the place was practically empty. My family's voices sounded louder than ever. And of course, they were still speaking Spanish.

I tried to hang back and pretend I didn't know them.

It took a few seconds for my eyes to

adjust to the darkness. That's when I noticed a group sitting back in the far corner. And I knew who they were.

It was my new friend, Lizzie, her parents, and her twin brothers. A few weeks ago, Lizzie's family moved into an old house down the block from us. When they first moved in, the Bully Twins had laughed and made fun of me when I spoke Spanish to Miguelito. It had made me boot-stomping mad. It had also hurt my feelings.

Quicker than Lizzie can climb up her jungle gym, I jumped behind Papi to hide. Lizzie had her back to the door. Maybe she wouldn't see us. I wasn't in the mood to talk to anyone — not even a good friend like Lizzie.

But Miguelito fixed that. "Gabí!Gabí!Gabí!" he screeched louder than an ambulance siren. He bounced and pointed. "It's Lizzie!"

I pulled away from Miguelito and jumped

behind a big potted palm. Lizzie spun around and spotted Miguelito. She ran over to him.

Mami, Papi, and Abuelita were busy choosing a pizza from the big menu board over the cashier. They didn't notice her.

"Hi, Miguelito," Lizzie said. "Where is Gabí?"

Miguelito covered his face with one hand and pointed toward me with the other. Then he ran off to hide behind Mami. He liked Lizzie, but he was still shy around her because he thought she was a "teenager."

I pretended I was checking out the leaves of the big potted palm and hadn't seen her.

"Hi, Gabí!" Lizzie hopped to my side. "Are you guys going to eat here?"

I forced a smile and nodded.

"Maybe your family could join mine and get to know one another," she said. "We could push two tables together. I have something I'm dying to tell you."

"Uh . . ." I began. "That would be really cool, Lizzie. But maybe some other time. We're . . . ummm . . . celebrating."

Lizzie's smile got even bigger. "Oh, yeah? What are you celebrating?"

"I . . . uh . . ."

"Gabí! Gabí! Gabí!" Miguelito yelled. "Come help us pick a pizza!"

"Oh," I said. "I'd better go. We'll join you next time, okay? I promise."

Lizzie looked disappointed. So I held up my pinkie finger in our secret superhero salute. She hooked hers to mine and grinned.

Whew! I thought. *That was close!*

Then I ran up to my family before Lizzie asked again what we were celebrating. No way could I tell her about my horrible, terrible, yucky, yucky day.

Luckily, Lizzie went to a different school than my other friends and I did. So if none of us told her, she'd never find out.

After Papi ordered, we sat down. Mami and Abuelita began laughing and speaking Spanish, as usual. They were talking about Mami's younger brother, Tío Julio, when he was a little boy. They said he was a lot like Miguelito.

Papi laughed and told a few stories about his own brothers in Argentina. When the pizza arrived, Papi helped Miguelito cut his slice in half.

Miguelito swung his legs and kept saying, "Um, ummm! *¡Qué bueno! ¡Más,más, más!* More,more,more!"

Their voices seemed *soooo* loud.

Louder than ever.

The little restaurant was shrinking by the minute.

I kept glancing at Lizzie's family. They were so quiet compared to my family. And every time my parents or Abuelita said something extra loud in Spanish, Lizzie's mom raised her eyebrows. Then she would look at Lizzie's dad and smile kind of weird.

I sank down in my seat.

Great! I thought. *I'll bet Lizzie's parents think Mami and Papi don't speak English!* They hadn't met my parents yet.

My stomach kind of flopped over. I felt a little queasy. For the first time in my life, I didn't like that my family spoke Spanish in public. I stared at them for a moment, then I looked back at Lizzie's family.

Next to Lizzie, her brother Jake (or maybe Jack) poked his twin. He pointed toward us and giggled.

I looked away and sank lower in my seat.

I could feel Jack's and Jake's eyes on us. And I could hear them giggling.

I forced myself not to look over at them. But out of the corner of my eye, I could tell something was happening at their table.

I couldn't stand it anymore. I glanced over.

Lizzie and her parents were talking about something, so they weren't paying attention. But — you won't believe this — the twins were watching us and waving their hands around. Like Mami and Abuelita were doing.

They were making fun of them!

My family and I use our hands a lot when we talk. Especially when we're having a good time. And Mami and Abuelita were having a really good time.

My face got superhot. My toes scrunched up in my shoes.

I wasn't sure if I was more angry or embarrassed. But I knew one thing: I was tired of being different! And I was tired of having a family that was different.

I wished I was wearing my cowgirl boots. My boots always make me feel like I can deal with anything. They're my secret weapon. Like my favorite superhero, Dragon-Ella, has her laser gaze.

But a couple of months ago, I got in trouble for threatening to kick Johnny. He was making fun of my Spanish then, too. Mr. Fine made me promise never to wear my boots to school again. He even sent my parents a note to tell them.

That's when Mami and Papi had a long

talk with me. They want me to control my temper. And my spunky feet. But spunky feet are hard to control.

Sometimes, they have a mind of their own. My foot kicked my chair.

Uh-oh! See? There they go again!

"What's wrong, Gabita?" Papi put down his slice of pizza.

I glanced at him, then I looked away. After a second, I looked back.

I cleared my throat. "Um . . . everyone, I have an announcement to make," I said in English.

For the first time since we walked into the restaurant, my family was paying attention to me. They put down their pizzas and stared.

"I've made a decision." I gulped, but I continued in English. "From now on, *no more Spanish!* I want to be like other kids. I'm only speaking English!"

I stomped my sneaker. Stomping made

me feel braver. But not as brave as my boots would help me feel.

Abuelita leaned forward. *"¿Cómo?"*

Oh, no! I thought. *I forgot about Abuelita. How am I going to stop speaking Spanish if she can't speak English?*

CINCO
CHAPTER 5
"A BIG POOH-POOH HEAD!"

"What do you mean, you're not speaking Spanish anymore?"

The next day at lunch, Devin practically choked on her tuna sandwich when I told her the news. We were sitting across from each other — way at the end of the long table, as far from our class as we could get.

"I'm just not! I don't want to anymore." I stomped a spunky foot.

Devin stared at me all squinty-eyed. It felt like she was trying to drill into my brain and figure out what I was thinking. "Does this have anything to do with what happened in class yesterday?"

"I don't want to talk about that." I sipped my Tooti-Frooti Joocie juice.

"It wasn't that bad, you know," Devin said.

Just then, we heard a loud snort, like a pig. Johnny and Billy walked up behind us carrying their trays.

"*Hola, enchilada,*" Johnny said, nodding at me. "*¿Chimichanga, cha-cha-cha?*"

"*Quesadilla de San José,*" Billy said. "*Olé.*"

They were all serious, like they were saying something that made sense.

I looked away and took another sip of juice, trying to ignore them.

"Watch it, Ga-*BEE*," Johnny said, "you'd better not drink too much."

Billy giggled. "You might not make it to the bathroom in time and then —"

"You'll *tinkle* in your pants — AGAIN! *¡Ay, ay, ay!*" Johnny screeched. He and

Billy cracked up. Then they sat at the other end of the table with their friends.

Heat shot from the tips of my toes to the ends of my hair. If I'd had my boots, I'd have fixed those nasty boys. They'd never order Mexican food again!

Instead, I glared at Devin, as if it was all her fault. "What happened yesterday wasn't that bad, huh? You think it's fun having Wiley the Smiley and his brainless buddy yelling Mexican food at you?"

I stomped my foot. "Nope, that's it! I'm *never* speaking Spanish again."

"But . . . but you can't just stop," Devin whimpered. "Who will I practice Spanish with?"

I shrugged. "I don't know. I don't care."

The moment I said that, I felt bad. Devin's lips turned down. She looked ready to cry.

At home, whenever I say, "I don't care," Mami reminds me of the little boy in that tiny book, *Pierre*. All he ever said was "I don't care." Then a lion ate him.

But that wasn't going to happen to me. The only person who heard me was Devin. And she was more like a kitty than a lion.

Still, I felt bad.

"I'm sorry," I said. "Maybe you can practice Spanish with your parents. It just can't be me. I won't speak Spanish anymore. I'd rather sniff stinky socks."

Devin shook her head. "I can't practice with my parents," she said. "They hardly speak *any* Spanish. They never learned that much when we lived in Panama. They say it's easier for kids to learn languages than it is for grown-ups."

Devin's family had lived in Panama for four years while her dad worked for an American company there. It was just before they moved here to Northern California.

"Hey, you guys!" Jasmine walked up with her tray and sat next to me.

She looked at Devin, then at me. "Okay, what's up? Why the faces?"

Devin crossed her arms in front of her chest. "Gabí won't speak Spanish with me anymore. Now I don't have anyone to practice with."

"Well, don't look at me." Jasmine picked up her fork and started to mush her spaghetti around. "All I know in Spanish is *hola* and *chévere*."

We taught Jasmine *chévere* a few weeks ago. It means "Cool!"

I sighed. "So you don't practice Spanish anymore, Devin. What's the big deal? *I'm* not going to speak it anymore. And I'm not going to miss it *at all*."

I stomped twice when I said "at all." *Stomp! Stomp!*

Devin took a deep, sad breath. "Well, I will."

"*I* sure won't miss it." Jasmine slurped some spaghetti. "I always feel left out when you guys start going at it in Spanish."

Devin gulped down the bite of sandwich she had in her mouth. "Sometimes, you make me so mad, Gabí! You're so stubborn — you won't back down even when you might be wrong. Don't you get how lucky you are to speak two languages?"

I snorted and glanced toward the other end of the table. Johnny and Billy were laughing. When Johnny saw me look at him, he mouthed something that looked like "*¡Cha-cha-cha!*"

I looked away. No, *Devin's* the lucky one. She doesn't have to feel bad about being different.

"Actually," Jasmine said, putting down her fork, "I've always been kind of jealous of you guys. I was thinking of taking Spanish, too, when we get to middle school."

I glared at Jasmine, like she was being a traitor or something. She shrugged and went back to slurping her spaghetti.

"What did your parents say when you told them?" Devin wanted to know.

I bit into my coconut cookie. "They thought I was kidding. But I wasn't. I meant it then, and I mean it now. *No more Spanish!*"

I stomped my foot again to show them.

"And how long do you think you can get

away with that?" Devin said. "You know how your parents are about rules and respect."

Jasmine nodded. "Devin's right, Gabí. Your mom's pretty strict."

"I'll figure something out," I mumbled.

But Devin shook her head. Slowly. Like she couldn't believe me.

"If you won't speak Spanish with me, I'll find someone else who will." Devin bit her lower lip, waiting for me to answer.

"Fine." I said. "See if I care."

Devin's eyes filled with tears. "Maritza Gabriela Morales Mercado, you're being" — Devin paused, like she was searching for the right word — "a big pooh-pooh head!"

Big pooh-pooh head? I thought. *She must really be upset. We haven't called anybody that since first grade!*

But before I could even try to apologize, Devin stood up. She stuffed the rest of her lunch in her bag, shoved back her chair, and marched off.

I was left sitting there with my mouth hanging open. Even Jasmine was speechless.

Devin and I have always been best friends.

This was our first *big* fight.

And all because of Spanish!

I felt like a lion had chewed me up and spit me out.

Even the lion didn't want me.

SEIS
CHAPTER 6
MEET POGO

"Hi, you guys!" Lizzie said that afternoon when Jasmine and I knocked on the door of the clubhouse in her backyard. She slipped out to join Jasmine and me, then real quick, she closed the door behind her.

I was glad her brothers weren't around. I didn't want to see the Bully Twins after the way they had made fun of my family at the restaurant yesterday. In fact, I never wanted to see the Bully Twins — *ever!*

Lizzie glanced around. "Where's Devin?"

"She said she had something to do after school today, so she couldn't make it."

Jasmine crossed her eyes. "She sounded very mysterious-a."

Sometimes Jasmine likes to pretend to speak Spanish by adding an *a* to the end of words. I rolled my eyes at her. This time she almost had it right. But I didn't correct her like I usually did. Spanish wasn't my problem anymore.

"Rat feathers!" Lizzie said. "Devin's going to miss my surprise. Maybe I should wait till she's —"

"No!" Jasmine and I yelled together. "Let's see it!"

Lizzie grinned. "Okay, I didn't want to wait, anyway."

"*Chév* — I mean, *cool*!" I did a happy hip-wiggle dance. "I love surprises."

Lizzie did a little skip-hop.

"I love surprises, too." Jasmine hip-wiggled like me. "Is it in the clubhouse?"

"Yup. Wait here a sec." Lizzie slipped back inside the clubhouse and closed the door behind her. In another second, she poked her head back out. "Ready?"

Before we could even nod, a large, squirming yellow dog pushed past Lizzie's legs. He jumped on me and licked my face. Then he jumped on Jazz and licked hers.

His tail was wagging so hard, I was afraid it would fall off.

"Pogo, sit!" Lizzie grabbed Pogo's leash and gave it a gentle tug.

Pogo sat.

His tail kept wagging. He grinned at us with his tongue poking out between his teeth. But he didn't budge.

"*¡Caracoles!* I mean, wow!" I said. "He obeys you."

"Yup." Lizzie grinned even bigger than Pogo. "Gabí and Jazz, meet Pogo. Pogo, shake hands."

Pogo lifted a front paw.

"Totally cool!" Jasmine bent over to shake Pogo's paw. "Is he yours?"

Lizzie nodded.

"Good dog!" Lizzie said and bent down to hug Pogo. "We just adopted him from a family who had to move and couldn't keep him. He's a golden retriever. He's already big, but he's only eleven months old."

I shook Pogo's paw. "You taught him these tricks all by yourself?"

"No," Lizzie said. "The family who had him first sent him to puppy school for obedience training. But we're going to do pet therapy together."

"Pet therapy?" I asked.

"I know what that is," Jasmine said. "It's when a pet is too hyper or sad and has to go to a pet shrink. Like people do."

"Really?" I scratched Pogo's ears. "He looks happy. And not too hyper."

Lizzie giggled. "It's not *that* kind of therapy. Pogo is such a smart dog, he's already an official Fluffy Friends pet-therapy dog. That means we get to visit people in the hospital and give *them* therapy. To make *them* happy. Get it?"

Jazz and I looked at each other. Then we looked at Lizzie and shrugged.

"Look." Lizzie knelt next to Pogo. "Sit next to us and stroke Pogo's fur. Okay, now play with his ears and let him lick your hand. How does that feel?"

Jazz and I smiled. "Very cool," we both said.

Lizzie nodded. "But having to be in the hospital is not so cool. And sometimes people get really sad."

"Is that how you felt?" I asked.

Lizzie had been in the hospital a couple of times to have surgery on her leg. Now she wears a splint to keep her leg straight. But nobody can see it because she almost always wears long pants.

At first, she didn't want anybody to know about it. But Miguelito and I found out by accident. After that, she said it was okay to tell Devin and Jasmine.

"Sometimes I got sad." Lizzie shrugged. "But being in the hospital wasn't all bad."

I wondered if that was true or if Lizzie was just being brave. I wouldn't like being in a hospital at all. But Lizzie doesn't want anyone to think she's a wimp.

"Now I get it," Jasmine said. "If I was in a hospital, away from my family, I'd be really sad. So a visit from Pogo would be double *chévere*."

"Yeah," I said. "Triple *chévere*, even! Uhhh . . . I mean, triple cool!"

Ugh! I thought. *Why do I keep slipping back into Spanish?*

Lizzie squinted at me. "Hey, Gabí, you're acting really weird. What's going on?"

Jasmine snorted. "Gabí refuses to speak any more Spanish."

Lizzie made a face like I'd snatched her last french fry. "No way! Why? I like to hear you speak Spanish."

I gave Jasmine a look meant to chill her bones. It told her: "Don't even *think* about telling Lizzie about that interview."

"It's no big deal, Lizzie, really," I said, ignoring Jasmine's crossed eyes. "Tell me more about Fluffy Friends. Can my cat, Tippy, and I do pet therapy?"

Jasmine rolled back on the grass, giggling at the thought of Tippy doing pet therapy.

"Don't laugh, Jazz," Lizzie said. "Tippy can do it. But he'll have to be able to walk on a leash and obey commands, so he won't run all over the hospital."

"That's all?" I jumped up. "Tippy can do that! Just watch! I'm going home to teach Tippy some new tricks. Right now!"

SIETE
CHAPTER 7
TRAINING TIPPY

"Here, Tippy,Tippy,Tippy!" Miguelito called. *"¡Misu!¡Misu!¡Misu!"*

When I got home, Miguelito was playing with Tippy in the front yard. He wanted Tippy to climb into a basket that he'd tied to the handlebars of his tricycle.

"Hey, Miguelito!" I held up a leash Lizzie had lent me. "Do you want to help me teach Tippy to walk on a leash?"

Miguelito gasped, real loud. He looked back at the house, as if he thought someone was watching us.

"Gabí, ¿por qué estás hablando inglés?" he

whispered. "You know Mami gets mad when we don't speak Spanish to each other."

"Because I want to . . . uh . . . to teach Tippy English." I knew I shouldn't make my little brother disobey our parents. So I added, "But you should keep speaking Spanish. You can translate for me, so Tippy will understand."

"Okay," said Miguelito, smiling real big. "Can I put the leash on him?"

"Only if you can catch him."

Tippy was trotting across the lawn, heading for the fence. I guess he knew something was up. Cats are kind of smart that way.

"Got him!" Miguelito pounced on Tippy before Tippy jumped on the fence.

"*¡Miaaaaaouurrrr!*" Tippy struggled to get loose.

I held Tippy while Miguelito clipped the leash to his collar.

The moment I set Tippy on the grass, he darted off. Then a second later — *SNAPO!* Tippy sprang back like a bungee jumper.

"*¡Miaouuuu!*" Tippy screeched. He shook his head, confused. And he started to pull and bite at the leash.

"Tippy, sit!" I said, the way Lizzie had commanded Pogo.

Tippy just rolled on his back and batted the leash with all four paws.

I sighed and stomped my foot. "Tippy, sit!"

Tippy began to walk backward, playing tug-of-war with the leash.

"Miguelito," I said, "tell him in Spanish."

"*Tipito, ¡siéntate!*" Miguelito sat down in front of Tippy. "*Así.* Like this."

"Sit, Tippy, sit." I pushed Tippy's rear down so he was sitting.

Tippy sat. But then he turned his head and closed his eyes, totally bored.

"Good, Tippy!" I said.

"*Muy bien, Tipito,*" Miguelito said. "Gabí, can we teach him to walk on the leash?"

"Okay." I gave the leash a gentle tug. "Tippy, heel!"

Tippy began to pull away and play tug-of-war again.

"*¡Ven, Tipito, ven!*" Miguelito repeated in Spanish.

I tugged a little harder. Tippy began to run in circles around me.

"Tip-*peee*!" I screamed. "Stop, Tippy, stop! *Stop,stop,stop!*"

But Tippy ran and ran until I was all wound up in the leash. My legs got twisted, and I almost tipped over.

"*¡Para, Tipito!*" Miguelito cried. "*¡Siéntate!*"

But Tippy didn't stop. And he wouldn't sit. Instead, he started running like crazy in the other direction.

Now I was free from being loop-de-looped in the leash.

Then Tippy yanked and pulled the leash from my hand.

"*¡Agárralo!*" I yelled. "I mean, get him, Miguelito!"

Miguelito and I hit the grass on our bellies at the same time. We tackled the leash. *SNAPO!* Tippy bungeed back.

"*¡Miaouuuu!*" Tippy screeched and shook his head.

I held the loop of the leash tight in my hand. "That's *meow* in English, Tippy. You'd better learn English, 'cause I'm *not* speaking Spanish *anymore*!"

I stood up and pulled Miguelito with me. "Okay, Tippy, heel!"

I tugged the leash again. Tippy pulled back. I pulled harder.

"*¡Te ayudo, Gabí!*" Miguelito held on to my waist. "I'll help!"

Now it was a real tug-of-war!

Miguelito giggled like this was the most fun he'd had in months.

But Tippy started sliding toward us. Then he put his head down . . . and his collar slipped right off his head!

I fell backward on top of Miguelito. We landed — *SPLAT!* — on the grass.

"*¡Caracoles!*" I yelled. "I mean, *snails*!"

Tippy flew across the lawn and disappeared over the fence.

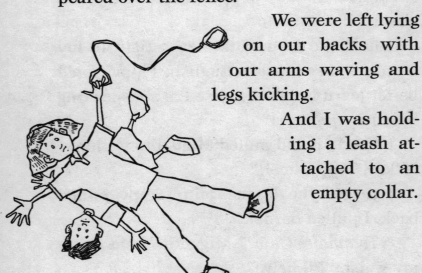

We were left lying on our backs with our arms waving and legs kicking.

And I was holding a leash attached to an empty collar.

<u>OCHO</u>
CHAPTER 8
WHAT ABOUT ME?

I left Miguelito outside playing and dragged myself to the kitchen for a snack. Training Tippy was hard work. And hard work makes me hungry.

"Devin!" I screeched when I walked in the door.

Devin and Abuelita were sitting next to each other at the kitchen table. They were all chummy-chummy, their shoulders practically touching.

"Why are you *here*?" I asked. "Why didn't you meet us at Lizzie's house?"

On the table in front of Devin sat a big plate of my favorite snack: guava paste and white cheese. Devin was even drinking my favorite drink: Malta, malted soda from Puerto Rico.

"Estoy ocupada." Devin popped a cube of cheese into her mouth. "I'm busy practicing Spanish with Doña Ela — um, with Abuelita."

I gasped. *"Abuelita?* You can't call her that! She's *my* grandma, not yours."

"Abuelita said I could." Devin turned to Abuelita and told her what she'd said — *in Spanish*. Abuelita nodded and patted her hand.

Devin gave Abuelita such a big smile that her braces showed. Devin *never* lets anyone see her braces.

Watching Abuelita pat Devin's hand the way she always patted mine made me feel kind of weird.

What was going on? Everything was backward. Abuelita was acting like Devin was her granddaughter. And Devin was acting like Abuelita was her best friend. *What about me? Where do* I *fit in?*

"Abuelita, *por qué* — why are you letting Devin call you that?" I asked her in English. "*I'm* your granddaughter."

Abuelita shrugged. *"Lo siento, Gabrielita. No entiendo inglés."*

I glared at Devin. I suddenly felt really mad at her. *Why is she acting like Abuelita is her best friend?* But I guess Devin misunderstood my look.

"Oh, I'm sorry, Gabí," Devin said sweetly. "You probably need me to translate for you. Abuelita said she's sorry, but she doesn't understand English."

"I do not!" I stomped my foot. "I *know* what she said. I can *understand* Spanish, I just don't want to *speak* it. I'd rather chew monkey chow!"

Devin took a sip of Malta. "That's too bad."

I stared at Devin for a second. *What's up with her? Devin never acts like this. She's almost . . . sassy, like Papi says I am. Maybe she's been hanging around me too much.*

"Well," I said, "if you want to speak Spanish so much, why don't you tell Abuelita what I said."

So Devin asked my grandma why she wanted to be called "Abuelita" by someone who is not her granddaughter.

Abuelita said it was because her granddaughter was a third grader who enjoyed her company and spoke Spanish. Right now, Devin was the only third grader who fit that description.

I felt about two inches tall. I was sad that Abuelita thought I didn't like spending time with her. But I couldn't give in and start speaking Spanish again. Not after everything that happened yesterday!

I don't want kids laughing at me because I speak a different language. I don't want to feel embarrassed like that again. Ever!

Devin turned to me and started to translate again. "Abuelita said it's —"

I stomped my foot and stopped her mid-sentence.

"Enough, already!" I felt silly having someone else speak for me, when I could speak perfectly well for myself.

I sat next to Abuelita and took her hand

in mine. "Abuelita, I love your company. And I love you. I just don't want to speak Spanish anymore."

Abuelita shook her head sadly. *"Lo siento, Gabrielita. No entiendo."*

Then — you won't believe this! — for the second time in one day, Devin went from being a kitty to a lion.

"Maritza Gabriela!" Devin stood up and scrunched her face at me. "You should be ashamed of yourself! How can you do this to your own grandmother? *¡Es una falta de respeto!* I know you don't need me to translate *that*!"

My jaw fell open. Devin was right. I was being disrespectful to Abuelita.

But I couldn't go back to speaking Spanish.

Not now. Not ever.

NUEVE
CHAPTER 9
"UM-UM-UMMM!"

"*¿Más tostones?*" During dinner, Abuelita offered me more crispy, fried green plantains.

Devin didn't stay. She'd already eaten: Devin-the-Lion had chewed me up and had *me* for dinner.

"Umm-hmmm," I answered, nodding with my mouth completely full.

I was avoiding speaking Spanish by nodding or shaking my head. And by keeping my mouth full. Another family rule is never to speak with your mouth full.

"*¿Quieres arroz y habichuelas, Gabita?*"

Papi started to pass the rice and beans, but Mami took the bowls.

"*Deja que ella misma lo pida, Antonio,*" said Mami. "If Gabí wants something, she knows how to ask for it."

Papi grinned at me and winked.

Mami raised an eyebrow. *"Gabí, ¿quieres arroz y habichuelas?"*

"Um-*hum*!" I popped a *tostón* in my mouth and nodded at Mami.

She mushed her eyebrows together. But she served me some rice and beans. "Another *bistec*?"

Mami knows how much I love Abuelita's special steak and onions.

"Mmmm." I nodded as I stuffed my face again. "Um-um-*ummm*!"

Mami gave me a strange look, like she was going to say something else. But before she could say a thing, Miguelito held up his plate.

"¡Más!¡Más!¡Más!" He swung his legs, asking for more.

"Shhh! *No grites*. Let's use our indoor voices," Mami said in Spanish. "Set your plate down."

When Miguelito set down his plate, he tipped over his glass of milk.

Milk splattered everywhere! Especially on Miguelito.

Mami took Miguelito to change. While Papi and Abuelita cleaned up the mess, I wolfed down the rest of my dinner.

Papi looked at my empty plate. "Gabita, are you done with your dinner?"

"Um-hum." I nodded.

"Do you have any homework left?" Papi sponged milk off the tabletop.

I shook my head. "No."

Papi stopped sponging and looked at me. "You're kind of quiet tonight, Gabita. Everything all right?"

I smiled and nod-
ded. "Uh-huh."

"Then why
don't you go
to your room
and read for
a while?" he
suggested.

"Okay." I hopped up and dashed to my room before Mami came back.

And before she could make me say anything in Spanish.

Because that was *not* going to happen. No way!

DIEZ
CHAPTER 10
FLUFFY FRIENDS DAY

"Is this the hospital you stayed in?" I asked Lizzie after her mom dropped us off near the main entrance.

It was a week after Jasmine and I had met Pogo. Somehow I'd managed to get through the whole week without speaking Spanish.

Jasmine, Lizzie, Pogo, and I walked up to a huge hospital building with big glass doors. This was Lizzie's and Pogo's first day of pet therapy together. Lizzie had invited Jasmine and me to tag along.

"Yup, I stayed up in Peeds," Lizzie said, leading the way. "That's hospital talk for

Pediatrics, the children's floor. That's where we're going now. All the kids will be waiting for us. Everybody loves pet-therapy day."

Jasmine raced ahead, then turned and watched Lizzie. "You and Pogo look *soooo* cool in your costumes."

"They're uniforms, not costumes." Lizzie held Pogo's leash so he stayed by her side. She really knew what she was doing. "We're working, not playing."

Pogo was wearing a green kerchief around his neck that read FLUFFY FRIENDS. Lizzie wore a matching green vest.

Around her neck, Lizzie wore a strap with a laminated picture hanging from it. It was a picture of Lizzie and Pogo wearing their uniforms. Below their pictures were their names.

"Sorry," Jazz said, crossing her eyes, "*uniforms*. I wish Devin were here to see you."

"She's too busy practicing *Spanish* with

Abu — my grandma," I mumbled. But I kept staring at the picture hanging from Lizzie's neck. "What's that, Lizzie?"

"It's our official badge. To show that Pogo and I are certified in pet therapy."

I looked down at my red cowgirl boots. They usually make me feel strong and important. But today, they weren't making me feel as important as having an official badge would make me feel.

Lizzie led us to a set of elevators, and we stepped inside. Pogo stayed next to Lizzie every step of the way.

"How's Tippy's training going?" Lizzie asked.

I groaned. "He'll never be able to walk with a leash as well as Pogo. I'm still trying to keep him *in* the leash. I don't think I can *ever* train him to be a good therapy cat."

Lizzie gave me a sad smile. "It's okay. Cats are hard to train. But you can still do pet therapy. Just join Pogo and me whenever we come here."

Lizzie looked so proud in her uniform, standing next to Pogo. She had a real job! She was doing good deeds by making sick kids feel better.

Lizzie and I always talk about our future jobs. Lizzie wants to draw comic book superheroes. She already made one up called Gecko Girl. I made up a superhero, too. Gabí the Great. (She's a lot like my favorite superhero, Dragon-Ella.) Gabí the Great fights crime.

That's *my* job — fighting bad guys. I've always thought stamping out evil was the most important thing in the universe. But now I wanted to *help* people, too.

Dragon-Ella fights evil *and* helps others. She catches the bad guys as Dragon-Ella. But she works with inner-city kids at night, after her regular job as a firefighter. She wants to make sure they won't grow up to be bad guys.

What good deeds could I do?

ONCE
CHAPTER 11
"NO PROBLEM-O!"

"They're here! They're here!" a boy yelled. "The Fluffy Friends are here!"

The moment the elevator doors opened, kids started gathering around us. Some were standing on their own. Some were on crutches. Some were being pushed in wheelchairs by nurses.

Two kids, a girl and a boy, were popping wheelies in their wheelchairs. When we stepped off the elevator, they raced down the hall toward us.

Most of the kids wore hospital gowns or pj's and robes.

"Okay, kids!" said a tall, skinny nurse. "Step back and let the therapists do their work."

The nurse walked up to us. She wore hot-pink hospital scrubs and had fuzzy white hair, like a Q-tip. "Hello. I'm Jane. You must be Lizzie. And you must be Pogo."

"Woof!" Pogo held up a front paw to shake hands.

Jane shook his paw. The kids said, "Oo-ooo!"

Lizzie smiled and nodded. "And these are my friends Jasmine and Gabí. They want to help, too."

"I see," Jane said. "Looks like Jasmine has already gone to work."

Jasmine was kneeling in front of a small girl in a wheelchair. Jazz was showing her how to cross her eyes. The little girl giggled.

"Hey," said the wheelie-popping boy, "I thought this was pet therapy, not *clown* therapy."

"Therapy's therapy." Jasmine crossed her eyes at him and smiled.

The boy crossed his eyes back.

Everyone cracked up.

"All right, kids," Jane called out. "Head to the crafts room. I've set up chairs so Pogo can visit with everyone individually."

The kids cheered and headed for a room down the hall.

Jane turned to us. "Not all of the kids can get out of bed," she said. "So when Pogo is done in the crafts room, I'd like him to visit those kids, too. Okay?"

"Sure," said Lizzie, grinning at me. "No problem-o!"

"Actually, I think that's 'no problem-*aaah*,'" said Jasmine. "Right, Gabí?"

I rolled my eyes. "Jazz . . ." I warned through clenched teeth.

Jane looked at Jasmine. "Do you speak Spanish?"

"Nope, not me." Then — *I couldn't believe*

it! — Jasmine pointed at me and said, "But Gabí does."

Jane gasped. She put her hands up to her chest, like she was covering her heart. "Oh, bless you! You're exactly the person we need."

Jane took my hand and started to lead me down the hall.

"Um . . . no . . . no, I don't —"

But Jane didn't hear me. She just kept dragging me down the hall.

I turned to look back at Lizzie and Jazz. I gave Jazz my chill stare. She and Lizzie just smiled real big and waved their fingers at me.

Pogo said, *"Woof! Woof!"* and doggie-grinned.

Traitors! I thought.

Jane led me into a big, sunny room with lots of hospital beds. All the beds were empty except one by the window.

A little boy with dark hair lay in the bed. He was looking at us.

"That's Pepito." Jane pointed. "He's here from Mexico to have several surgeries done on his spine. Pepito is very lonely because he only speaks Spanish. None of the other kids speak Spanish. And the nurses are too busy to spend much time with one patient."

Jane shook her head sadly. "Could you visit

with him for a little while? Maybe you could tell him a story."

I looked down and rubbed the toe of my boot on the icky-green linoleum. I couldn't look into Jane's eyes.

"Uh . . . I don't really speak Spanish . . . anymore. I used to, but . . ."

Jane sighed. "Oh, I see. Well, I had so hoped . . ."

I kept rubbing the linoleum with my boot. "I'm really sorry."

"If you don't remember how to speak Spanish, it's not your fault," Jane said. Then she snapped her fingers. "I have an idea! Why don't you sit with Pepito for a little while? Maybe some Spanish will come back to you."

"Oh, I couldn't —"

But Jane took my hand and led me to the side of Pepito's bed.

I dragged my eyes from my boots to the boy's face.

Pepito seemed only a little older than Miguelito. His shiny, dark hair and big brown eyes reminded me of my little brother. But Pepito's eyes were sad.

"*Hola, Pepito.*" Jane put her hands on my shoulders. "This is Gabí. *Gabí habla español*" — she held her thumb and pointer finger together — "*un poquito.*"

The moment she said that, Pepito's sad eyes brightened.

I looked back down at my boots.

"Here, Gabí." Jane brought me a chair. "I'll leave you two alone to visit."

Before I could say anything else, she was gone.

I glanced at Pepito. *Here is my chance to do a good deed*, I thought.

But the question is, can I do it?

DOCE
CHAPTER 12
DOING GOOD DEEDS

"Me gustan las botas." Pepito told me that he liked my boots.

I nodded and smiled. I took off one boot and held it up so he could see it better. I had cleaned and shined them last night. I didn't want to wear grubby boots to a hospital.

My boot gleamed. The polish showed off the white stars and curly half-moons that were carved into the red leather.

Pepito held up a finger. He traced the edges of a white half-moon.

"¿Eres vaquera?" He wanted to know if I was a cowgirl.

I giggled and shook my head no.

"*¿Hablas español?*"

Do I speak Spanish? *Do I?* I used to. *Why did I ever stop?*

I shrugged. Pepito sighed, and his eyes got sad again. He turned his head and stared out the window.

I looked at my beautiful red boot.

I didn't deserve to wear these boots. These boots were meant to help people and to stamp out evil. I wasn't doing either. I was worse than the bad guys I wanted to fight!

Here was a little boy who needed my help. And I was just making him sadder. Mami and Devin would be ashamed of me. *I* was ashamed of me.

If only there were something for me to fight in this room. Something that would make me deserve to wear these boots. Something that could help Pepito.

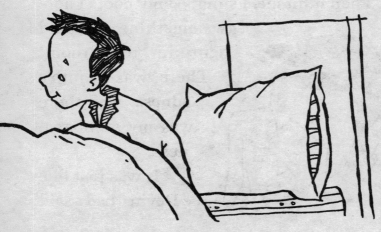

I slipped the boot back on my foot. I stood up and began to walk slowly from the room.

Then I heard something. *Was that a sniffle?*

I spun around. Pepito had his face turned away from me. *Was he crying?*

Oh, no! What should I do? What would Dragon-Ella do? Would she walk out on a sad little boy in a hospital? Could she?

No way! I decided. She'd rather hold hissing hornets in her bare hand! So would Gabí the Great. And so would I!

Then it hit me. I stomped my boot. There *was* something I could fight in this room! There was Pepito's sadness. And there was my stubbornness.

It was just like Devin had said

in the school cafeteria: I was being a big pooh-pooh head.

¡Caracoles!

I stomped again. *Stomp! Stomp! Stomp!* Hard and loud.

Pepito wiped his eyes and turned his head toward me.

"*Sí, Pepito, hablo español.*" I grinned real big. It felt good to speak Spanish again. And it made me feel strong — like my boots make me feel when I first slip them on.

Pepito's eyes brightened, and he grinned back.

"*¿Y sabes qué más?*" I asked if he knew what else. "*Soy una* big pooh-pooh head."

"Big pooh-pooh head?" Pepito looked puzzled.

I nodded. "It means *una gran boba* in English," I replied in Spanish.

Pepito giggled, and I giggled. And I kept doing and saying silly things to keep him giggling. And I said them all *in Spanish*!

Then, you won't believe what happened next!

The wheelie-popping boy appeared in the doorway.

"Hey, you guys! Come listen to this!" he said, waving to the others. "Gabí is making Pepito laugh."

He popped another wheelie and rolled toward us. The wheelie-popping girl followed close behind. And with her came all the other kids. Lizzie, Pogo, Jasmine, and Jane were the last to enter.

"Hi, Gabí. I'm Brett," said the wheelie-popping boy. "And this is Amy."

Amy was the wheelie-popping girl. "How did you get Pepito to laugh?" she asked. "He never talks to anybody. Do you speak Spanish?"

"Of course she speaks Spanish," said Brett. "How else could she do it? We haven't been able to talk to him or cheer him up no matter what we tried."

"None of us speak Spanish," Amy said, balancing herself on her back wheels. "Would you tell Pepito our names?"

"Yeah," said Brett, "and maybe you could teach us a few words in Spanish. So we can talk to him sometimes."

I gulped. Speaking Spanish to one lonely little boy was one thing. But speaking Spanish in front of a group of English-speaking kids . . . I remembered how Johnny and Billy and the Bully Twins had made fun of my Spanish.

I looked at Jane. She winked. Jasmine smiled and crossed her eyes.

Lizzie held up her little finger in our secret superhero salute.

Pogo said, "*Woof!*" and doggie-grinned.

If Devin had been here, she'd have given her hair a double tug.

¡Caracoles! I looked down at my boots. *Am I going to be a big pooh-pooh head forever?*

I stomped my boot. *No way! I'd rather hug a warthog!*

"Sure, Brett," I said. "Want to know how to say 'big pooh-pooh head' in Spanish?"

Everybody roared with laughter.

I taught the kids some words in Spanish for a while. Then I translated so they could talk to Pepito.

It felt really good to speak Spanish again and to be helping others. I felt important. And *soooo* proud! I didn't even need an official badge.

Next, we had Pogo jump on a chair so he could visit with Pepito. Pogo lay his head on Pepito's chest while Pepito stroked Pogo's soft ears.

Pepito smiled and smiled. And his eyes were all shiny and happy.

While Pogo did his pet-therapy thing, I translated so the kids could keep talking to Pepito. And also, so Pogo could understand Pepito. Because unlike Tippy, Pogo doesn't speak Spanish.

At least not yet.

TRECE
CHAPTER 13
¡SORPRESA!

The moment I got home from the hospital, I ran to the kitchen. Devin was there again, practicing her Spanish with Abuelita.

"Lo siento, Abuelita." I gave her a big hug.

"Lo siento, Devin." I hugged her, too. "I'm so, *so* sorry I refused to speak Spanish to everybody. I was being *una gran boba.*"

Devin smiled so big her braces showed. "Welcome back, Gabí."

Abuelita held my face and kissed the tip of my nose. "You weren't a big silly," she

said in Spanish, "you were just confused. Everybody gets confused sometimes."

I nodded. "Super-confused. I thought if I stopped speaking Spanish, I could be like everybody else. Then nobody would make fun of me."

I sat next to Abuelita. "But all I was doing was turning my back on my family . . ." I said. "And on people who needed me, like you and Devin. I just didn't like being different. But I guess sometimes being different is a good thing."

"*Ahhh,*" Abuelita said, "very wise words. What made you realize all that?"

"I met a little boy today." I smiled. "In the hospital. His name is Pepito."

I went on to tell her all about Pepito and Pogo and Lizzie and pet therapy. "I felt really bad at first because I couldn't do pet therapy with Tippy. Then I found out that I could do *people* therapy, just by using my Spanish."

"Es verdad," Abuelita said, nodding. "It is true. Like your *mami* always says, speaking more than one language is a powerful thing."

"Sí, el idioma es muy poderoso. Now I have two secret weapons — my boots and my Spanish. But one of them is always with me. Like Dragon-Ella always has her laser gaze. And no one can take it away . . . not unless I let them."

Abuelita patted my hand. "Perhaps one day, I can learn some English. Your *abuelito*, before he died, had wanted me to learn English. But I was always too busy. . . ."

"¡Chévere, Abuelita! I can help you," I said. "And I'd like to help Pepito learn some English, too. He's really lonely, and it makes him sad. So I promised to visit him again tomorrow. And I promised I'd bring a surprise."

I told Abuelita and Devin about the surprise. "Can you help me with it?"

Abuelita laughed and clapped her hands. *"¡Qué linda sorpresa!* Of course I will help. It's a delightful surprise!"

"Me too!" said Devin. "And I know exactly how I can help."

So the next day, Abuelita, Miguelito, and I took a bus to the hospital. Devin wanted to come with us, but her mother needed her home early.

"Hola, Pepito," I said when I walked into the big room with all the beds. I was wearing my red boots and a red vest. *"¡Aquí está tu sorpresa!"*

I gave the leash I was holding a double tug. I showed him his surprise.

Miguelito bounced into the room. He'd been waiting in the hall until I gave him the signal. He wore a black-and-white cat costume. It was a costume that Devin had worn for Halloween one year. It was a little big, but with Devin's help, Abuelita was able to make it fit.

A hood with cat ears covered Miguelito's head. Devin had painted his face black and white with whiskers. She even painted a black spot under Miguelito's chin, like the one Tippy has.

Miguelito wore a red kerchief around his neck that matched my vest. On the kerchief, I'd painted white letters that read CAT THERAPY.

"*¡Sorpresa!*" I yelled. I did my happy hip-wiggle dance.

The moment they saw him, the other kids in the room cheered.

"*Éste es mi gato, Tippy.*" I led Miguelito-Tippy to Pepito's bed. "He's a therapy cat.

And he's very unusual. Tippy is a talking cat. And the very best part of the surprise is that Tippy speaks Spanish."

I said all this to Pepito in Spanish. Then I turned to the other kids and translated. "And for you guys, Tippy can even speak English."

They all yelled, "Oo-oooo!" and clapped.

"*¡Miaouuuu!*" said Miguelito, like a Spanish-speaking cat would. Then he translated for the other kids. *"Meowww!"*

Miguelito bounced up to Pepito and shook his hand. *"Hola, Pepito."*

Everybody cheered again.

Once each child had visited with Miguelito-Tippy, I went to get Abuelita.

"This is Abuelita, my grandma," I told everyone in English. (Miguelito translated for Pepito.) "She's going to tell us a story from Puerto Rico. That's where she's from. But she only speaks Spanish, so Tippy and I will translate."

Abuelita waved to everyone. She'd wanted to wear something fun, too. So she borrowed Mami's favorite *pava* — her traditional Puerto Rican straw hat.

Abuelita sat next to Pepito. She patted his hand and began her story.

"Había una vez, y dos son tres . . ."

Abuelita always starts her stories that way. It means "There was one time, and two makes three . . ." It sounds kind of goofy in English, but it works in Spanish. And Abuelita only speaks Spanish.

At least for now . . .

¡HABLA ESPAÑOL!
(That means: *Speak Spanish!*)

abuelita/o (ah-booweh-LEE-tah/toh): grandma; grandpa

¡Agárralo! (ah-GAH-rrah-loh): Get him!

arroz (ah-RROHS): rice

así (ah-SEE): like this

¡Ay! (EYE): Oh! An expression of alarm, surprise, or pain

ayudo (ah-YOO-doh): I help

baile (BY-leh): dance

bistec (bees-TEHK): beefsteak

boba (BOH-bah): silly girl

botas (BOH-tahs): boots

¡Caracoles! (kah-rah-KOH-lehs): "Yikes!" or "Wow!"; also means, "snails"

chévere (CHEH-beh-reh): Cool!

¿Cómo? (KOH-moh): What?

cucaracha (koo-kah-RAH-cha): cockroach

entiendo (ehn-TEEYEN-doh): I understand

español (ehs-pah-NYOHL): Spanish

estoy ocupada (ehs-TOY oh-koo-PAH-dah): I'm
  busy

Es verdad (ehs vehr-DAHD): It is true.

falta de respeto (FAHL-tah deh rehs-PEH-toh):
  a disrespectful act

familia (fah-MEE-leeyah): family

gallina (gah-YEE-nah): hen; chicken

gato (GAH-toh): cat

habichuelas (ah-bee-CHOOWEH-las): kidney or
  navy beans

habla (AH-blah): he or she speaks

hola (OH-lah): hello

idioma (ee-DEEOH-mah): language

inglés (een-GLEHS): English

linda (LEEN-dah): pretty; adorable; delightful

lo siento (loh SEEYEN-toh): I am sorry

mami (MAH-mee): mommy

más (MAHS): more

me gusta (meh GOOHS-tah): I like

misu (MEE-soo): an expression used mostly by
  Puerto Ricans and Cubans that means, "Here
  kitty, kitty, kitty!"

montones (mohn-TOH-nehs): oodles; a lot

muy bien (moowee beeyen): very good

no entiendo (noh ehn-TEEYEN-doh): I do not understand.

no grites (noh GREE-tehs): don't yell or shout

¡No más! (noh MAHS): No more!

No te oigo (noh teh OEE-goh): I can't hear you

número (NOO-meh-roh): number

¡Olé! (oh-LEH): Ta-da!

¡Para! (PAH-rah): Stop!

perdida (PEHR-dee-dah): lost

poderoso (poh-deh-ROH-soh): powerful

poquito (poh-KEE-toh): little bit; small amount

¿Por qué? (pohr KEH): Why?

problema (proh-BLEH-mah): problem

¿Qué? (KEH): What?

¡Qué bochorno! (KEH boh-CHOHR-noh): How embarrassing!

¡Qué bueno! (KEH BOOWEH-noh): Yummy!

¡Siéntate! (SEEYEHN-tah-teh): sit down

sorpresa (sohr-PREH-sah): surprise

soy (soy): I am

tapón (tah-POHN): traffic jam
tapones (tah-POH-nehs): traffic jams
todavía (toh-dah-VEE-ah): still
vaquera (bah-KEH-rah): cowgirl
¡Ven! (vehn): Come here.

#4 Please Don't Go!

Abuelita tells the best stories ever!

"Y *colorín, colorado, este cuento está acabado,*" Abuelita said. That's the way she always ends her stories. It's just a long, silly way to say, "The end."

"You're the best storyteller in the whole wide world, Abuelita!" Miguelito said. "I could listen to you tell that story a trillion jillion times."

He must be a mind reader, because I was thinking the same thing.

I sat up on my knees and hugged Abuelita as hard as I could. "Me too!"

"OOFF!" Abuelita said, laughing. "*¡Qué abrazón!*"

I sat back on my heels and took her hand. "Abuelita, promise me something," I said, squeezing her hand. "Promise that you'll never, ever leave us. Promise that you won't go back to Puerto Rico, and you'll stay with us forever. Promise."

"*Sí, Abuelita, ¡promételo!*" Miguelito began to bounce on the bed. "Promise!Promise!Promise!"

Abuelita patted my hand and gave us a sad smile. "Don't you think you'd get tired of your old *abuelita*?"

"Never!" we both cried at once, bouncing on our knees. "Promise! Promise! Please! Pleeeeease!"

"*¡Shhh, niños!*" Abuelita laughed. "We'll see."

But the smile faded from my face, and I stopped bouncing with Miguelito.

"We'll see" is what grown-ups say when

they really mean: "No, but I don't want to argue about it."

Abuelita can't leave us! I was just getting used to having her around!

There had to be something I could do to make her stay.

I'm Gabí the Great. I was sure I could think of *something*.

But what?

MEET
Geronimo Stilton

A REPORTER WITH A NOSE FOR GREAT STORIES

Who is Geronimo Stilton? Why, that's me! I run a newspaper, but my true passion is writing tales of adventure. Here on Mouse Island, my books are all bestsellers! What's that? You've never read one? Well, my books are full of fun. They are whisker-licking-good stories, and that's a promise!

www.scholastic.com/kids

■SCHOLASTIC

GERS